Está nublado
It's Cloudy

Celeste Bishop

traducido por / translated by
Charlotte Bockman

ilustrado por / illustrated by
Maria José Da Luz

PowerKiDS press™

New York

Published in 2017 by The Rosen Publishing Group, Inc.
29 East 21st Street, New York, NY 10010

First Edition

Managing Editor: Nathalie Beullens-Maoui
Editor: Sarah Machajewski
Book Design: Michael Flynn
Spanish Translator: Charlotte Bockman
Illustrator: Maria José Da Luz

Cataloging-in-Publication Data

Names: Bishop, Celeste.
Title: It's cloudy = Está nublado / Celeste Bishop.
Description: New York : Powerkids Press, 2016. | Series: What's the weather like? = ¿Qué tiempo hace? | In English and Spanish. | Includes index.
Identifiers: ISBN 9781499423211 (library bound)
Subjects: LCSH: Clouds–Juvenile literature.
Classification: LCC QC921.35 B57 2016 | DDC 551.57'6–dc23

Manufactured in the United States of America

CPSIA Compliance Information: Batch #BS16PK: For Further Information contact Rosen Publishing, New York, New York at 1-800-237-9932

Contenido

Contents

Hoy no puedo ver el sol.

I can't see the sun today.

Está nublado.

It's cloudy.

Cuando está nublado,
el cielo está lleno de nubes.

When it's cloudy,
the sky is covered with clouds.

Algunas nubes son blancas y esponjosas.

Some clouds are white and puffy.

¡Parecen almohadas!

I think they look like pillows!

Otras nubes son oscuras y planas.

Other clouds are dark and flat.

Estas nubes son una señal de que va a llover.

These clouds are a sign of rain.

Las nubes se han oscurecido.
Creo que va a llover.

The clouds are getting darker.
I think it's going to rain.

Mi mamá dice que puedo jugar fuera hasta que empiece a llover.

My mom says I can play outside until it rains.

Me pongo mis botas
de agua por si acaso.

I wear rain boots
just in case.

Las nubes tapan el sol.
¡No puedo ver mi sombra!

The clouds hide the sun.
I can't see my shadow!

Las nubes se han oscurecido aún más.

También hace mucho viento.

The clouds are getting darker.

It starts to get windy, too.

Es hora de entrar.

It's time to go inside.

Mamá dice que los días nublados son perfectos para leer.

My mom says cloudy days are perfect for reading.

El día se mantiene nublado.

It stays cloudy all day.

¿Qué tiempo hará mañana?

What will the weather be
like tomorrow?

Palabras que debes aprender
Words to Know

(las) almohadas
pillows

(la) lluvia
rain

(las) botas de agua
rain boots

Índice / Index